A Hat for MINERVA LOUISE

Janet Morgan Stoeke

SCHOLASTIC INC. ■ New York Toronto London Auckland Sydney

■

For Colin Wilcox Brooks

■

ISBN 0-590-98405-5

12 11 10 9 8 7 6 5 4 3 2   6 7 8 9/9 0 1/0

Printed in the U.S.A.   08

First Scholastic printing, December 1996

Minerva Louise loved snowy mornings.

Her friends didn't like them one bit.

They stayed inside all day with their heads tucked under their wings.

Not Minerva Louise. She couldn't
wait to go out exploring.

Everything was so beautiful!

She wanted to stay out all day.
But it was too cold.

If I had some warm things like you,
she said, I could stay out and play.

A scarf might help.

But not this one. It's way too big.

And these shoes are too big, too.

A hat! That's just what I need.

But not this one.

And not this one, either.
It's too heavy.

There must be a hat around
here somewhere.

Minerva Louise looked outside.
Everyone had on a fluffy white hat!

Oh, *your* hat is wonderful!
Where did you get it?

Oh, look! What's over here?

A hat! It's perfect. But what's this?

Oh, it's two hats!

Which was just fine

with Minerva Louise.